DISCARDED

DAILY PRISON LIFE

Crime and Detection series

CRIME AND DETECTION

DAILY PRISON LIFE

JOANNA RABIGER

MASON CREST PUBLISHERS
www.masoncrest.com

Mason Crest Publishers Inc.
370 Reed Road
Broomall, PA 19008
(866) MCP-BOOK (toll free)
www.masoncrest.com

First printing

1 2 3 4 5 6 7 8 9 10

Library of Congress Cataloging-in-Publication Data on file at the Library of Congress

ISBN 1-59084-384-3

Editorial and design by
Amber Books Ltd.
Bradley's Close
74–77 White Lion Street
London N1 9PF
www.amberbooks.co.uk

Project Editor: Michael Spilling
Design: Floyd Sayers
Picture Research: Natasha Jones

Printed and bound in Malaysia

CONTENTS

Introduction

From the moment in the Book of Genesis when Cain's envy of his brother Abel erupted into violence, crime has been an inescapable feature of human life. Every society ever known has had its own sense of how things ought to be, its deeply held views on how men and women should behave. Yet in every age there have been individuals ready to break these rules for their own advantage: they must be resisted if the community is to thrive.

This exciting and vividly illustrated new series sets out the history of crime and detection from the earliest times to the present day, from the empires of the ancient world to the towns and cities of the 21st century. From the commandments of the great religions to the theories of modern psychologists, it considers changing attitudes toward offenders and their actions. Contemporary crime is examined in its many different forms: everything from racial hatred to industrial espionage, from serial murder to drug trafficking, from international terrorism to domestic violence.

The series looks, too, at the work of those men and women entrusted with the task of overseeing and maintaining the law, from judges and court officials to police officers and other law enforcement agents. The tools and techniques at their disposal are described and vividly illustrated, and the ethical issues they face concisely and clearly explained.

All in all, the *Crime and Detection* series provides a comprehensive and accessible account of crime and detection, in theory and in practice, past and present.

CHARLIE FULLER

Executive Director, International Association of Undercover Officers

Left: A prisoner looks out at the world mournfully from a traditional solitary cell. Many new prisons are under construction throughout the U.S., and new architectural forms are rapidly being introduced to the system.

The U.S. Prison System

The U.S. prison system is the largest in the world and the most complex. Instead of a single national system, it is made up of a network of prisons run by the federal government, state governments, and local governments or municipalities. The U.S. also has the largest prison population in the world. Many states across the U.S., as well as the federal government, are currently constructing new prisons. Because of this continuing expansion of the prison system, the U.S. now has some of the most modern and technologically advanced prisons in the world.

The U.S. prison population first began to rise during the 1980s and early 1990s. During this period, North America experienced the effects of a profound economic **recession**, high unemployment, and soaring crime rates. Drugs and gangs were major causes of concern, and urgent action was necessary to combat the new **epidemic** of crack cocaine addiction and gang-related activity. The president at the time, Ronald Reagan, declared a "War on Drugs," and the criminal justice system in the U.S. became accordingly "tough on crime." As a result, more people were sent to prison for drug-related offenses. The state of California led this change in 1994 with a harsh law that stated, "Three strikes and you are out."

This law meant that anyone convicted of three **felonies** might end up facing life in prison. A felony offense is categorized as a serious crime, while a **misdemeanor** is a less-serious crime. For example, occasional shoplifting is generally considered a misdemeanor, while car theft is more often

Left: Inmates at a "boot camp" in Georgia perform a military-style drill. "Boot camps" are a special type of short-term prison program used mainly for the rehabilitation of younger offenders. For those who may never have worked or held down a steady job, "boot camps" provide an opportunity to develop a sense of personal responsibility.

An inmate leads a discussion in a drug rehabilitation group meeting at a state prison in Montana. Most inmates have a history of drug and alcohol addiction problems. Effective drug and alcohol rehabilitation programs form an essential part of nearly all prisons' daily routines.

classified as a felony. Though the measure is considered controversial, many other states have followed the example of California and tightened their drug violation laws so that they are empowered to remove persistent offenders and gang members from the streets of the larger American cities.

Because some U.S. prisons are currently overcrowded, a vigorous program of prison construction is underway. As the U.S. prison system has grown, so have state governments, and the federal government increasingly turned to security specialists. Private security companies, such as

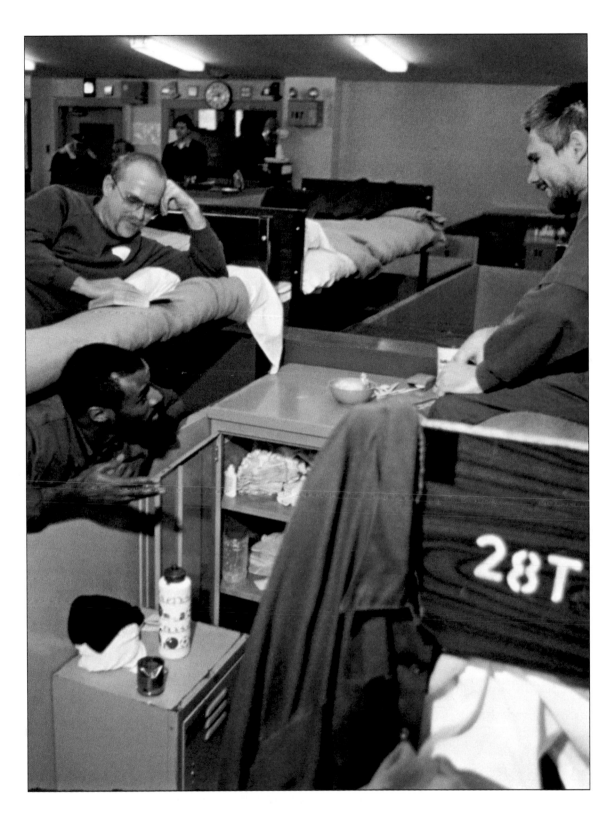

In some older U.S. prisons, overcrowding is now a major problem. Building new prisons, and modernizing prison design, is essential to house the rising prison population. Large dormitories are common in older low-security prisons and sometimes sleep as many as 100 inmates.

Corrections Corporation of America (CCA) and Wackenhut Corrections Corporation, now manage several major prisons in the U.S. The federal government or a state government hires these organizations on a conctractural basis, and their prisons are subject to the same inspections and standards as state-run and federal-run prisons.

THE U.S. FEDERAL PRISON SYSTEM

Founded in 1891, the U.S. federal prison system is the oldest prison system in the U.S. Federal prisons **incarcerate** violators of federal law. Examples of

After a disruptive incident at a correctional facility in Connecticut, armed police patrol the perimeter. During periods when there is an increased potential for rioting, guards are on high alert and the prison perimeters will be more heavily guarded than usual.

AVERAGE FEDERAL SENTENCE

OFFENSE	MEAN	MEDIAN
All offenses	56.8 months	33.0 months
All felonies	58.0 months	36.0 months
Violent felonies	63.0 months	Not applicable
Drug felonies	75.6 months	55.0 months
Property felony—fraud	22.5 months	14.0 months
Property felony—other	33.4 months	18.0 months
Public order felony—regulatory	28.0 months	15.0 months
Public order felony—other	46.5 months	30.0 months
Misdemeanors	10.3 months	6.0 months

Source: U.S. Department of Justice, Bureau of Justice Statistics, Federal Criminal Case Processing, 2000—With Trends 1982–2000 (Washington, D.C.: U.S. Department of Justice, November 2001)

federal law violations include **racketeering**, certain types of fraud, **money laundering**, **conspiracy**, smuggling, drug trafficking, and immigration law offenses. Although a national system, the federal prison network is only the third-biggest prison system in the United States. In fact, Texas has the largest prison system in the world, and the second largest is California.

The federal prison system has 86 federal facilities and contracted facilities throughout the United States. The federal Bureau of Prisons (BOP) is responsible for managing the entire federal prison system. The BOP central office is located in Washington, D.C., and answers to the Department of Justice. The Bureau of Prisons is divided into six regions: the Mid-Atlantic, the North Central, the South Central, the Western, the Northeast, and the Southeast. There are between 13 and 20 prisons in each individual region, and a regional director is responsible for each facility in his or her region. Because the federal prison system is currently overcrowded, prisoners are not always housed in their home region. This means that family members may be forced to travel out of state in order to visit them, sometimes having to travel across the entire country.

Federal prison facilities are organized in bands, classified as minimum security, lower security, high security, and maximum security. Inmates are classified according to the length of their sentence. An individual with 30 years remaining to serve on his sentence must be held in a **penitentiary**. A person who has 20 years remaining to serve may not be held in a facility rated lower than medium security. A person who has more than 10 years to serve may not be held in a facility rated lower than low security. Once a prisoner is considered to be within 10 years of his or her release date, he or she may be held in a low-security prison camp. Most people in federal prisons have committed some kind of drug-related offense, and every federal prison includes some kind of drug-rehabilitation program.

STATE PRISON SYSTEMS

The rest of the U.S. prison system is managed by individual states, according to their particular laws and policies. This means that the prison system as a whole in the U.S. is immensely varied. Louisiana currently has the highest total incarceration rate, with more than one percent of the state's population incarcerated. California has the largest number of people in prison of any state. Texas has the highest number of modern, privatized prisons and admits a large number of prisoners from other states. States with large prison populations are Georgia, New Mexico, Nevada, Arkansas, Alabama, Florida, South Carolina, Virginia, and Maryland. It is important to remember that these are states with some of the poorest and least well-educated populations. Indeed, about 70 percent of the prison inmates in the United States are illiterate, which is why many prisons run education programs and encourage inmates to gain qualifications.

Administrated by local police, the county jail has long played a vital role in the U.S. prison system. Jails provide holding cells for convicted offenders facing trial and also house prisoners who are being transferred from one prison to another.

An inmate at a "boot camp" is intimidated by his drill instructor. Boot camps are usually for first-time offenders and aim to "shock" the young inmates into a sense of personal responsibility by subjecting them to punishing physical activity and militaristic daily routines.

Many states favor rural locations for new prisons, partly for reasons of space, but also as an attempt to provide local rural communities with employment. In New York, for example, most inmates are from the New York City area, but many will be incarcerated miles from their home communities in prisons situated in depopulated rural upstate New York.

JAILS

In addition to federal, state, and private prisons, the U.S. has approximately 3,300 jails managed at the local level. Jails generally confine inmates sentenced to one year or less, although this varies from state to state. Jails also hold people who must be incarcerated pending "arraignment" (a word meaning the first appearance in court in front of a judge by someone who is accused of a criminal charge), trial, conviction, or sentencing. Those who have been returned to custody for violating the terms of their release on **probation** or **parole** are often sent to jail. Jails also house those who are being transferred from one correctional authority to another or who are in transition between prison institutions. Nearly one-third of all U.S. inmates are held in jails operated by the county sheriff's departments, city police, or other local-level law enforcement agencies.

INTENSIVE SHOCK PROGRAMS

During the 1980s, state and federal prisons began to develop intensive "shock" prison programs known as "boot camps," usually for young, first-time offenders. The first boot camps in the U.S. were opened in Georgia and Oklahoma in 1983. Since that time, more than 50 other facilities have been set up in 33 states, aiming to prevent young people from re-offending.

Boot camps are eligible only to those serving a sentence of 12 to 30 months and aged between 17 and 35. Inmates who are eligible must be serving a first incarceration sentence or have a minor history of prior incarcerations. No offender believed to pose a security risk or who has a poor disciplinary record is admitted, and violent offenders are rarely allowed to attend. Boot camps are not compulsory, but voluntary, and many inmates consider them a preferable option to the full sentence in prison. By attending a boot camp, offenders have the chance to reduce their prison sentences.

A boot camp-style program generally lasts between 90 and 180 days and follows an intensive training model based on the military style of physical

Inmates at a Georgia "boot camp" line up outside their cell blocks. Because "boot camps" are lower-security prisons, they are currently used only for offenders who have been sentenced for nonviolent offenses and who are not considered to present a security risk.

rigor and discipline. Each state has a slightly different **regimen**, but nearly every camp features barracks-style housing, military titles and uniforms, drills, platoons, and military-style disciplinary action and punishments.

DIFFERENCES BETWEEN STATE AND FEDERAL BOOT CAMPS

FEDERAL SYSTEM	STATE SYSTEM
Average age: 27	Average age: 19-20
No reduction in sentence	Reduction in sentence
No punishments	Punishments
Rehabilitative	Military style
Guaranteed transfer to halfway house	No transfer to halfway house, but parole may be reduced

Boot camps also emphasize rehabilitation and educational, vocational, and life-training skills. These include communication skills, social and personal responsibility development, self-restraint and anger control, victim awareness, self-esteem development, sex education, and parenting skills. It is worth noting that counseling for substance abuse and treatment is a major element of most programs.

The sparse living conditions and emphasis on physical and verbal abuse of boot camp attendees remain controversial, and the effectiveness of the programs has attracted both media and academic attention, much of it negative. However, many argue that boot camps improve self-esteem, as well as physical and mental

Self-help and behavioral classes, such as anger management and life values, are encouraged in most prisons. Here, an inmate-taught class discusses personal effectiveness, enabled by a relaxed and informal group atmosphere in which everyone is allowed to speak.

THE U.S. PRISON SYSTEM

- The U.S. sends its people to prison at the highest rate per capita of all Western nations. In other words, the percentage of its population that the U.S. sends to prison is higher than the percentage of its population of any other country that incarcerates its own people, including countries with large prison systems, such as Russia and China. Recent figures suggest the U.S. incarcerates five times as many people per capita as Canada and seven times as many as most European democracies, such as England, France, and Germany.

- U.S. gun homicide rates run 20 times the rate in comparable nations, such as England and France.

- The U.S. punishes less-serious or nonviolent offenses more frequently and severely than other nations, who primarily reserve prison for serious or violent offenders. In the U.S. federal prison system, one in five prisoners is a low-level, drug-law violator with minimal or no prior criminal history.

- Most people admitted to prison or jail serve short sentences for minor crimes. Indeed, 87 percent of offenses nationwide in the U.S. are nonviolent.

health, by bringing about a radical change in lifestyle and by forcing offenders to rise to challenges they may never have faced before. Many offenders who have experienced a boot camp regimen comment on the opportunity to push physical, mental, and emotional limits to new extremes. All of this serves to boost self-confidence, giving many inmates a belief in themselves for the first time in their lives. A major difference between ordinary prisons and boot camps is that camps encourage teamwork, while in most prisons "doing your own thing" is the rule. Staffing levels at boot camps are also higher than in prisons, offering inmates more individual attention and opportunities to develop skills.

The federal Bureau of Prisons has two "shock incarceration facilities": the Intensive Confinement Center (ICC) for men at Lewisburg, Pennsylvania, and the Intensive Confinement Center for women at Bryan, Texas. ICC Lewisburg is designed to incarcerate 192 adult male federal offenders. ICC Bryan is designed to hold 120 adult female offenders in dormitory-style barracks.

GENDER AND MENTAL HEALTH ISSUES

The U.S. prison system generally treats male and female inmates equally, but separates the sexes entirely. Male and female prisoners are not housed within the same institution, although some male and female prisons are located within close proximity. A major issue for women prisoners is pregnancy and birth. Women inmates do give birth in prison, but they are not allowed to keep their babies within the prison system. The children of these incarcerated women must therefore be cared for either by relatives or legal guardians or, if necessary, by the state.

Psychiatric prisons exist for offenders who are proven to be severely mentally ill. In such institutions, medication is enforced and rehabilitative care is compulsory. Isolation units may be used periodically to separate violent psychiatric offenders and are sometimes used to prevent suicide attempts or self-inflicted bodily harm.

As the U.S. prison system continues to expand, many new programs have been introduced and technological advances made. Overcrowding is decreasing as new prisons are built, and as a result of innovations in prison architecture and technology, the U.S. prison system continues to modernize itself at a dynamic rate.

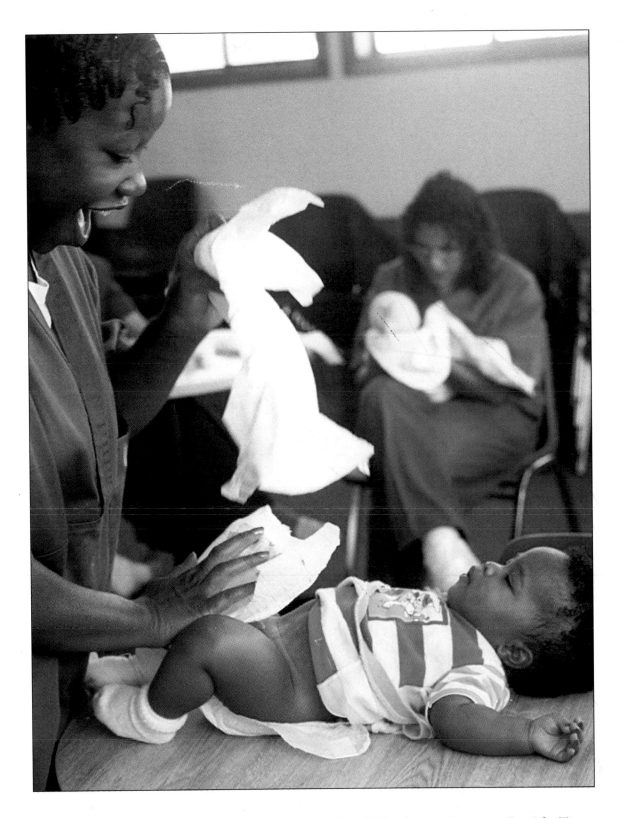

An incarcerated mother changes her son's diaper during visiting hours at a correctional facility in Colorado. Incarcerated mothers are not permitted to raise children within the prison walls and spend limited—and therefore precious—time with them.

A Typical U.S. Prison

Prisons in the United States vary greatly, according to the time at which they were built, their location, and their security level. For example, the Louisiana State Penitentiary at Angola is the largest maximum-security prison in the United States and houses some 5,000 men. It employs approximately 1,800 people and owns extensive farmland in the area. The oldest prison in the U.S., Leavenworth United States Penitentiary in Kansas, is the largest federal maximum-security prison, holding approximately 2,300 inmates. Other prisons have been converted from former military barracks—for example, Fort Dix in New Jersey. Older prisons, such as Folsom State Prison near Sacramento, California, may be Gothic structures with cells stacked five stories high. In contrast, however, nearby New Folsom Prison is a modern, futuristic prison design, reflecting modern concerns about prisoner welfare.

The classic U.S. prison design is a **tiered** building designed around central staircases. All prisons have a general housing unit, which includes an office for the housing unit manager, laundry rooms, and separate rooms for watching television, an exercise room with gym equipment, and a series of telephones for inmates to use. Most prisons have some kind of medical wing, where inmates with medical problems are assigned, and an administrative area for the offices of the unit manager, case managers, and counselors who make up the unit team.

Some prisons have single-unit cells housing one or two inmates only, while other lower-security facilities have dormitories designed to sleep

Left: A Death Row inmate is escorted in handcuffs on his way to the shower. In order to ensure the safety of correctional officers and other prisoners, Death Row inmates are always handcuffed when moving from their cells to other areas of the prison.

Typical traditional prison cell block architecture: note the narrow corridors, designed to channel the flow of inmates in orderly single file, and a layout that provides guards with a clear view of every level, thus enabling them to maintain control.

groups of 10 or 12. In the dormitories are military-style metal bunk beds and wall lockers in which each prisoner keeps all of his or her belongings. Most prisons have heat in the winter, but do not have air conditioning. Most prisoners prefer cells with two inmates because they allow for greater privacy. In some prisons, two-inmate cells are available only to prisoners who are nearing the end of their sentences and who have earned points in the good behavior credit system.

THE CONTROL CENTER AND THE PERIMETER

Today, prison security relies heavily on modern technology and extensive computerization. In the newest prisons, access to a cell is controlled

Prison inmates relax in a Texas prison recreation area. Inmates are encouraged to exercise and to socialize quietly during recreation periods. For many, this is the highlight of their day, giving them the opportunity to socialize, but it is also a time of increased risk for outbreaks of violence.

electronically from a booth overlooking the housing unit. A centralized command center at the heart of the prison is known as the control center, and monitors and controls inmates' movements, prison gates, cells, cameras, and alarm systems. The control center also receives calls from around the prison and sends out help according to the request. For example, if an inmate reports a severe headache, the housing unit manager may call the control center and a physician will be sent to examine the inmate immediately. The control center also takes emergency calls from corrections officers when they require backup or assistance. Security cameras are widely distributed throughout modern prisons and these play a vital role in monitoring prisoner movements and activities.

Perimeter control is another important aspect of daily federal prison life. Mobile patrol officers drive fast, well-equipped vehicles along the prison boundaries looking for signs of attempted escape. The mobile patrol officer is heavily armed and always wears a bulletproof vest. He or she also frequently checks the computer alarm system and links to the control center. Some prisons have special watchtowers along the perimeter fence, and a few newer prisons even have motion detectors built directly into the fence. Not all prisons have watchtowers: although a highly efficient means of surveillance, they are costly to maintain and require considerable extra levels of staffing, which is not always available.

THE SPECIAL HOUSING UNIT

Nearly all prisons have a special housing unit in which violent inmates are contained. The safety of prison staff is the highest priority in the special housing unit, and it is closely monitored by the control center at all times. Inmates here often require at least three guards to supervise them and must be handcuffed every time they are moved, even when simply going to the bathroom or shower. Inmates in the special housing unit are not permitted to work in the prison kitchens or workshops, and are only allowed into recreation areas in small, closely supervised groups. Sometimes, this

In Huntsville, Alabama, an armed prison guard watches over a line of prisoners who are part of a chain gang, as they march out to work in nearby fields.

Supervised by an instructor, inmates learn valuable computer skills in a Texas prison. Gaining such vocational skills means that prisoners are more likely to find gainful employment after release and less likely to return to crime.

housing unit is used to house prisoners, such as sex offenders, who may require special protection from other inmates.

THE FOOD SERVICE

The food service is where inmate crews help prepare food and meals are served. The food service provides three meals a day and broadly resembles

Work provides inmates with a sense of purpose and with opportunities to build on basic skills and to demonstrate good behavior. Here a woman inmate is seen at work in a fiber-optics factory at the Federal corrections facility in Danbury, Connecticut.

An adult education teacher at an Illinois boot camp inspects a student's work. Most inmates lack basic literacy and many do not have their GED. As well as improving future employment chances, study improves concentration and confidence as part of general inmate rehabilitation.

a cafeteria. Some inmates prefer to use food vendors that the prison provides, and in lower-security prisons, inmates are even allowed to use microwaves to prepare simple, ready-made meals. In the food service, inmates are closely supervised at all times by a number of staff because mealtimes are considered a time of increased security risk.

WORKSHOPS AND WORK ASSIGNMENT AREAS

All prisoners, except those in maximum-security facilities or with a history of violence, are encouraged to work and to lead productive lives. Inmates may either work in general maintenance, alongside trained professionals, or in special workshops that vary according to the product the prison produces. Many prisons stamp license plates, repair office equipment for state agencies, or repair and build furniture for state offices. Much prison work entails manual labor and tools. These must be carefully managed to prevent inmates from stealing objects that could be used in an escape attempt or to overpower a corrections officer or another inmate.

THE EDUCATION DEPARTMENT

Education programs are in progress day and evening in all prisons. A wide range of classes and group workshops are available. Many classes focus on improving self-esteem, controlling drug dependency, and on developing empathy for victims and increased personal responsibility. Inmates without high school diplomas are encouraged to prepare for their General Equivalency Diploma (GED) or for more advanced national educational programs to increase their employment opportunities when they are released. All prisons contain a library and computers for inmate use, and every prisoner is encouraged to develop vocational skills. Sometimes, courses are also available from a local community college. Other prisoners offer arts and crafts activities. Prison ministries also work with inmates on a voluntary basis to provide Bible study classes, prayer and reflection, and spiritual guidance and support.

PRISON STAFF

Prison staff include a wide range of personnel, from corrections officers, accountants, nurses, and laundry workers, to records specialists, secretaries, and paralegal secretaries. Prisons are in operation 24 hours a day, 365 days a year, and most correctional officers work shifts with sometimes as little as eight hours off between each shift. Prison staff are constantly on their feet, and must be extremely vigilant at all times. Various members of staff must perform head counts and **inventories**. For example, the food service foreman is responsible for counting the inmates and checking them against computer-generated photographic IDs. He or she must also account for all cutlery and kitchen equipment after every meal has been prepared and served. Every staff member is responsible not just for security within the prison, but also for each other's well-being.

Prison staff are highly trained to respond appropriately to prisoner hostility, disobedience, or to a general threat of violence. They must be alert at all times and must get to know inmates' habits and tendencies in order to monitor any attempts to smuggle goods, knives, or drugs in and out of the institution. Prison staff are not permitted to become too friendly with inmates, and close relationships are actively discouraged.

Professional electricians, carpenters, plumbers, and others, known as mechanical services staff, are responsible for daily upkeep in prisons. Mechanical services staff members also train inmates as apprentices in a given trade—carpentry, for example. The apprenticeship program helps prepare inmates for life outside prison and encourages them to take an active role in the upkeep of the institution.

Although U.S. prisons vary greatly in their location and their architectural design, most follow a similar routine and set of rules and guidelines. Before an offender can be admitted to prison, he or she must first be assessed and classified in order to determine what level of security is appropriate and therefore what type of treatment he or she will receive. This aspect of the prison system is discussed in the following chapter.

COURSES OFFERED IN PRISON

- Courses in basic literacy and study for the GED
- General educational values
- Degree programs through local community colleges
- Early childhood development
- Vocational courses, such as welding, electronics, fire science, photographic technician training, nursing, hospitality, library assistant, and legal assistant
- Courses in computing and technology
- Psychology courses in anger management, parenting skills, substance-abuse support groups, and group counseling
- Drama and art therapy (in a limited number of prisons)
- Bible study and prayer groups

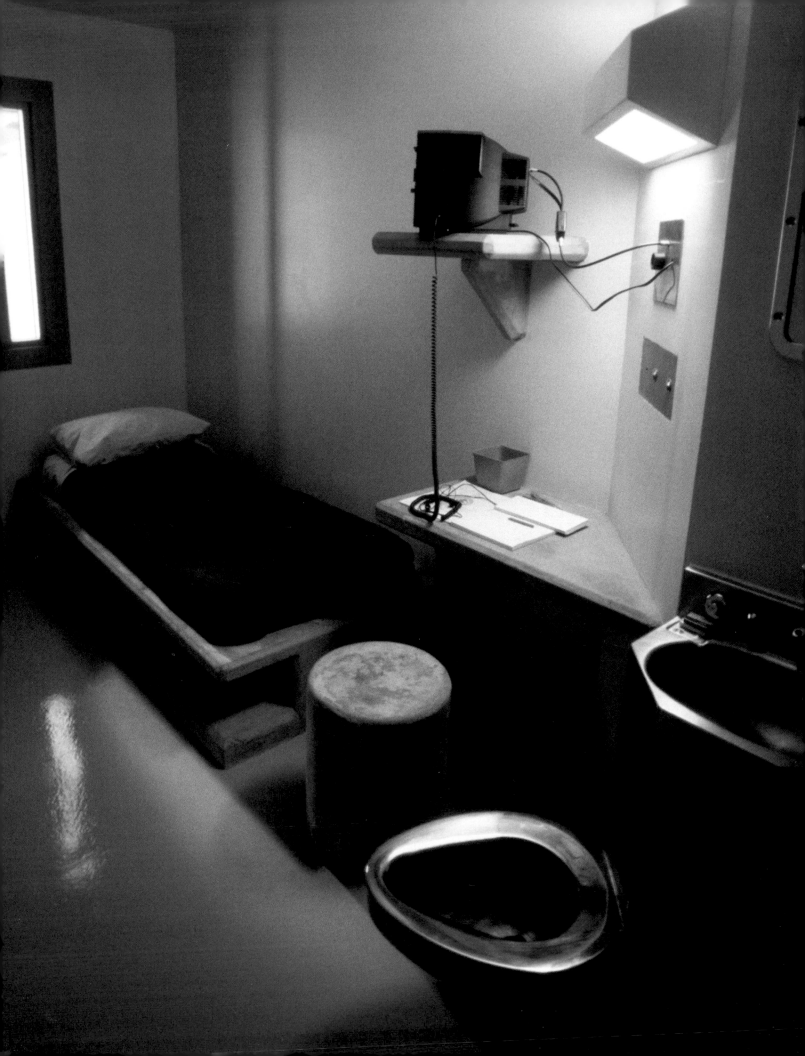

Prison Admission and Classification

Soon after the trial verdict, the sentenced criminal may ask his or her lawyer to request a specific prison institution—for example, a prison that family members can easily reach by car or public transportation. Although federal and state prison systems recognize that family visits are important to inmates' rehabilitation, overcrowding in prisons sometimes prevents prison authorities from placing inmates in institutions that are easily accessible for family members. For most, prison therefore means severely reduced contact with family members. Indeed, family ties may often break down as a result, particularly between incarcerated parents and their children.

Prisoner classification takes place in a detention center known as a reception center or a reception diagnostic unit, sometimes while the inmate is held in a county jail. In federal cases, the sentenced criminal is supervised during this waiting period by the Pretrial Services Department. In the case of state prisoners, the appropriate State Department of Corrections is responsible. The inmate's public or private defender's records are crucial during this stage because they provide the reception center staff with a complete picture of the offender's crime and background.

Upon entering the federal or state reception center, the new inmate receives an *Admissions and Orientation Handbook* in which the major prison

Left: A solitary confinement cell at a maximum-security federal prison. Solitary confinement is necessary for violent inmates, for those who are persecuted by prison gangs, for certain sex offenders who may be bullied by other inmates, and for those on Death Row.

Inmates admitted to a "boot camp" program fold their newly issued prison clothing. "Boot camp" programs test inmates to the limit. In return for undergoing this intensive and often stressful training, successful inmates are permitted to move directly to parole.

rules are listed. This booklet contains information on classification, rules governing inmate conduct, discipline, visiting, mail, counts, **commissary**, and other such issues. New inmates are usually required to sign a receipt, which means agreeing to abide by all the rules and regulations contained in this booklet—and therefore accepting punishment for failing to do so.

The time taken to process new inmates in the reception center depends on the availability of staff members and the number of incoming prisoners. Generally, the immediate intake process takes between one and four hours. However, the entire admissions and orientation process generally takes from 30 to 90 days. If a prisoner has special problems, such as a medical history or disability or a mental health record, the admissions procedure may be delayed even further. During this time, new prisoners receive a physical examination, a psychological evaluation, educational assessment, and a substance-abuse evaluation.

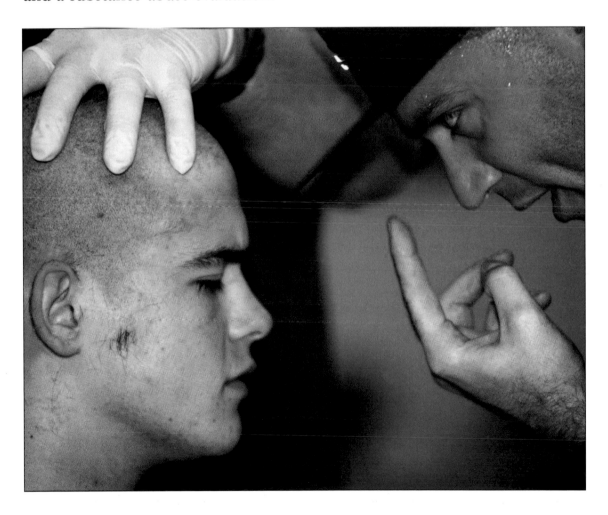

A new "recruit" at an Illinois "boot camp" has his head shaved while a corrections officer interrogates him on the nature of his crime and his feelings about it. "Boot camps" often use shaming tactics to "shock" inmates into a sense of increased personal responsibility.

THE SCORE SHEET

Most prisons, state and federal, use a uniform classification system in the form of a "score sheet" designed by a classification committee composed of prison staff. Points are awarded or deducted depending on specific factors in the inmate's legal case; in other words, according to the nature of the crime and the circumstances under which it was committed, and according to previous criminal history and background. The number of points awarded determines the appropriate security level in as objective and scientific a fashion as possible. Length of sentence is an important factor in deciding where a convicted felon will be placed. The kind of prison where the inmate will eventually be incarcerated also depends on both the nature of his or her crime and on the inmate's previous history. In the U.S. prison system, there are three custody levels, or levels of prison security.

The first kind of prison is high, or close, security. This is reserved for those who are serving long-term sentences or who have an escape history or who are considered prone to violence. Close-custody inmates must be maintained within an armed perimeter or under direct armed supervision when outside of a secure perimeter.

The second category is the medium-security prison, for those who may have a considerable amount of prison time to serve, but are generally less likely to behave antagonistically, and who have a lower escape risk. Medium-custody inmates do not require armed supervision when outside a secure perimeter, but they require direct sight and sound supervision.

The third category is the minimum-security prison, for those who are usually within two years of release, who are generally nonviolent and compliant, and who do not represent an escape risk. Minimum-custody inmates are eligible to be outside of a secure perimeter without sight and sound supervision. Minimum-custody inmates are checked periodically, but do not require a staff member to be present at all times. They may even be based at a special low-security work camp away from the main institution while awaiting parole.

Guantanamo Bay, a U.S. Naval base and high-security prison in Cuba, where terrorist detainees, such as members of the Al Qaeda group, are held for questioning.

MORE CATEGORIES FOR CLASSIFICATION

Other factors in the classification process include what is known as the prisoner's "stability," meaning his or her emotional stability and ability to interact, perform tasks, and reason. The prisoner's stability is assessed according to his or her age, marital or common-law relationship status, high school graduation record, and recognized trade or profession and employment history.

Military service is a positive determining factor in some states. Past behavior—good or bad—in other institutions in which the inmate may have previously been incarcerated is taken into account. Special case factors include medical problems or restrictions, enemy situations (for example, cases in which an already incarcerated prisoner may pose a threat), gang affiliations, and special work skills (a special skill in carpentry, for example, may be more in demand at one prison than in another). These factors are

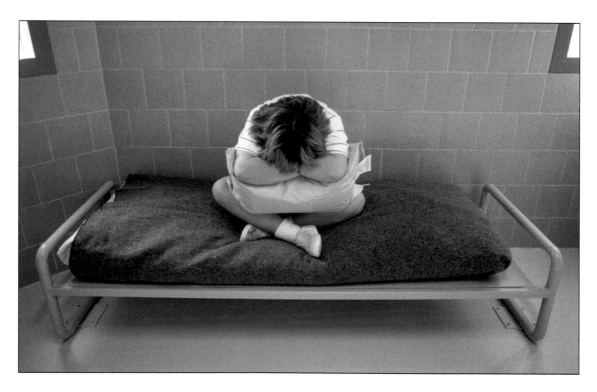

A teen prisoner in Texas showing signs of emotional distress. Admission to prison often entails a long period of isolation and uncertainty: new inmates are vulnerable to bullying, and may encounter problems caused by not knowing the unspoken rules that govern inmates' behavior.

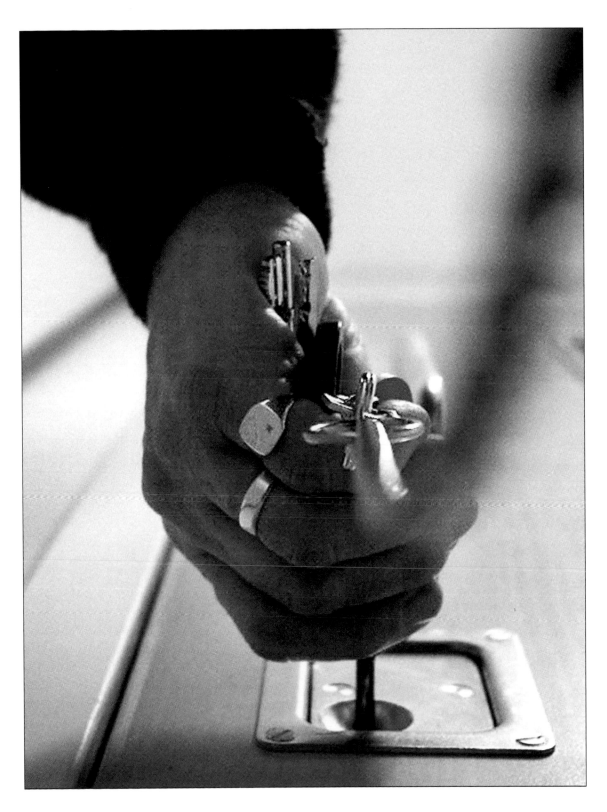

At the end of every day in a prison, each officer's key must be accounted for—prison security is all-important and can never be compromised. Just one missing key may mean that every single lock throughout the facility has to be changed.

A sentenced criminal may be sent to a particular prison because his or her job skills match the kind of work available there. Here, inmates craft and assemble hospital chairs. Although work is not compulsory, it is encouraged, not least to prevent boredom.

usually subject to an administrator's individual judgment rather than a points system (which, by definition, is generalized).

As soon as a new inmate is classified and an institution is designated, he or she is allocated a number in the state or federal prison system, and is then assigned to an institution and housing unit. When inmates receive their housing assignments, they are also assigned to a unit team, usually consisting of a unit manager, case manager, and correctional counselor. The unit team works with the inmates to address any problems they may encounter and is also ready to answer any questions.

There are few privileges in the reception center, and new inmates are isolated from the outside world. In many states, the unclassified prisoners are not allowed visitors or phone calls, although they are allowed to receive letters. The inmate awaiting classification and placement is not eligible for work or for any form of credits or earnings within the prison system.

The newly classified inmate is taken to the designated prison—high, medium, or minimum security—under armed guard. Incoming prisoners are advised to avoid the emotional drain of saying good-bye to loved ones and family members at the prison gate.

SETTLING IN

Usually, if the institution uses an inmate telephone system, the new prisoner will be able to make calls within about three business days of his or her arrival at the prison, after his or her telephone account has been activated. Once they have settled in, new prisoners generally find people from their hometown or people of similar backgrounds, who help them to adjust and find their way around and teach them some of the rules of the institution. New prisoners are vulnerable and stand out from the crowd. They are usually ignorant of unspoken inmate rules and codes and of gang activity. Corrections officers watch carefully for any signs of bullying or exploitation, and a prisoner can request a change of housing unit or work assignment should difficulties arise.

As soon as the new inmate is assigned a job according to his or her skills and reliability, he or she will work within the prison to earn money in order to purchase items such toiletries and extra food items. New inmates may choose from a wide variety of educational and sports activities, and are encouraged to take skills-related courses in practical subjects, such as wood- and metalwork. Family members may send new inmates money orders in order to help them buy extra items, but personal checks are generally not accepted, and sending cash by mail is discouraged. Inmate accounts are managed within the prison system.

The new inmate must adjust to the unfamiliar sights, sounds, and experiences of the prison institution and may undergo considerable stress and depression during this initial period, especially if undergoing drug- or alcohol-dependency rehabilitation. New inmates must also learn to negotiate an often-hostile social atmosphere in which harassment, bullying, gang activity, and verbal abuse are commonplace.

From high up in a fortified watchtower, an Arizona corrections officer watches Death Row prisoners as they are marched out to work in nearby farmers' fields.

FEDERAL PRISON POPULATION 2000

- Forty-one percent of federal felony defendants were charged with a drug offense.
- Thirty-three percent were charged with a public-order offense.
- Seventeen percent were charged with an immigration offense.
- Nine percent were charged with a weapons offense.
- Twenty-one percent were charged with a property offense.
- It is estimated that 50 percent of the current population in federal prisons are those serving time for drug-related violations.

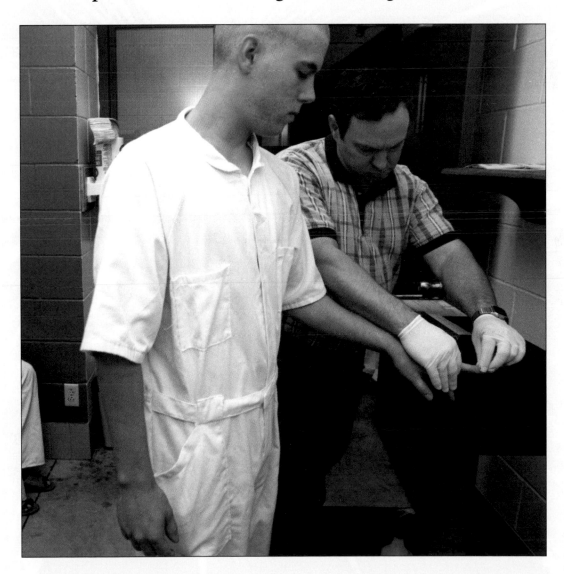

Daily Routine

In most state or federal prisons, inmates are awakened early, between 5:30 A.M. and 6:30 A.M., by a cell-house whistle. At the sound of the whistle, inmates must get out of bed, wash (men must also shave), get dressed, make their beds, and clean their cells before leaving for the day. Most prisons insist that inmates maintain a degree of order and cleanliness in their daily lives, and untidy cells or an unwashed or unkempt appearance often results in the loss of privileges, such as telephone access or visitation rights.

There is a second morning whistle some 40 minutes after the first, and at this point, cell doors are opened. Inmates must stand in an orderly fashion outside their cells while they are counted. Inmates are then marched into the dining area or mess hall for breakfast. Here, they line up in numbers by order of their cell tier or floor level and another count is performed. Inmates usually seat themselves in the dining area or mess hall in cell order.

Breakfast is served in most prisons at 7:00 A.M. Prisoners are allowed to help themselves to as much food as they like, or they use a ration card system in which set portions are given to them. Inmates are allowed to talk quietly during meals, but raised voices and rowdy behavior are strictly forbidden. Inmates who are considered troublesome by the authorities must eat their breakfast alone in their cell, and for some inmates, privacy and silence at breakfast time is preferred.

Breakfast usually lasts about 20 minutes, and afterward inmates are expected to display their knives and forks prominently on their trays so correctional officers can count silverware for each place setting. In this way,

Left: "Boot camp" inmates stand in a highly orderly fashion outside their cells, awaiting the daily early morning count and to receive their work assignment for the day.

Juvenile offenders wait in line in a juvenile correctional facility cafeteria. Mealtimes are heavily supervised by correctional officers: disruptive or disorderly behavior is strongly discouraged and can result in punishment or additional sentence time.

corrections officers ensure that no knife or fork has gone missing. Inmates who are assigned to work in the kitchen that day will remain behind as kitchen crew to clear up, do dishes, and help prepare the midday meal. Others line up to receive their work assignments for the day.

WORK ASSIGNMENTS

Inmates with work assignments in prison industries and workshops are led to the recreation yard, where they are lined up according to the area of work they will undertake that day—in the laundry, clothing shop, furniture, glove or shoe workshop, garden, or field. Inmates who do not have a work assignment that day are led back to their cells by order of tier. They may attend education classes instead. Most inmates work every day, with time set aside for recreation and education or counseling.

Manufacturing state license plates is one of the more traditional prison work assignments available in the U.S. Prisons provide the U.S. with many valuable products.

U.S. PRISONERS AND THE VOTE

There are 3.9 million Americans who cannot vote because they were or are prisoners. Of that figure, 1.4 million are African-American males and as a result, 13 percent of black men in the U.S. have no vote.

The laws of 48 states impose disenfranchisement for all prisoners and former prisoners. In Virginia, for example, in 1996 and 1997, only 404 former prisoners had the right to vote reinstated, out of 200,000 ex-convicts. Only Maine and Vermont impose no restrictions on inmates or former inmates.

Security in the work areas is extremely tight because different inmates are in contact with one other and come into contact with potentially dangerous objects. Inmates selected to work must file into their respective assignments through a metal detector. As soon as they reach their duty post, correctional officers count the inmates. Work usually begins at 7:30 A.M., and inmates have a short break at 9:30 A.M., when they are allowed to smoke in designated areas. A prison whistle calls them back to their work assignment, and they continue working until 11:30 A.M.

Then the prison's whistle signals the end of the work period and inmates again line up and pass through the metal detector. After inmates have put down tools from the workshops and other supervised work units, staff members carefully count the tools. They pay close attention to prisoners leaving the workshop to make sure that no dangerous objects or tools, which might enable them to escape, have been taken. Dangerous chemicals and liquids are closely monitored and safely stored under lock and key.

Before entering the mess hall for lunch, all prisoners are counted again. The midday meal is served in the mess hall at around 11:40 A.M. in most prisons and is heavily supervised. The lunch period generally ends at noon, when inmates again must display their knives and forks and are lined up and marched back to their cells for the noonday count. After this count, they are locked up in their cells for a short break and a chance to relax, free from the supervision of correctional officers.

At 12:20 P.M., inmates assigned to work are marched back to the recreation yard, where correctional officers count them again. They start work again at 12:30 P.M. and take another eight-minute break at 2:30 P.M.

AFTER THE WORKING DAY ENDS

In most prisons, the working day ends at 4:15 P.M., when inmates are again marched to the recreation yard and lined up to be counted. After the count, inmates are allowed to receive their day's mail.

Basketball is a popular prison sport and provides a healthy aerobic workout and an opportunity to relax after a hard day's work in prison workshops.

At this point, those inmates who are not on work assignment are released from their cells and marched into the dining hall for the evening meal. Food must be closely supervised to prevent theft because some inmates may try to help themselves to an extra portion. Meals that contain popular foods, such as fried chicken, must be closely monitored for this reason. Once again, knives and forks must be displayed and counted.

Most prisons provide educational opportunities. Inmates' efforts at self-improvement are generally encouraged and may even result in a reduced sentence.

Inmate crews, meanwhile, clean up the dining room and sweep the floor, and all inmates are thoroughly searched after such kitchen duties.

For most inmates, recreation takes place at this stage, after the day's work is over. In the recreation yard and gymnasium, trustworthy, nonviolent inmates play sports like basketball, lift weights, or work out. Competitive sports, such as wrestling or boxing, are generally not allowed, but pool and table tennis are common indoor activities. Recreation is a time of increased risk for outbreaks of violence or attempts to escape, and correctional officers are watchful. At the same time, recreation is the highlight of the day for inmates and provides them with a social and physical outlet, as well as a chance to stay in shape and be healthy.

They are also allowed to make 10-minute telephone calls, one at a time, to parents or friends, usually around 6:00 P.M. In order to use the telephone system, prisoners must first be assigned a Personal Identification Number (PIN) from their unit teams. These are collect calls, meaning that the person they are calling must accept the responsibility of paying for them, and are usually limited to four 15-minute calls a day. Only a prescreened and approved list of numbers may be called, and this is programmed into the prisoner's personal prison system phone account. Any abuse of the phone system, such as three-way calling, is subject to severe punishment and even extra years of sentencing.

TIME FOR SELF-IMPROVEMENT

At 8:00 P.M., many inmates choose to enter the education department to take part in the numerous self-improvement programs the prison has to offer. All kinds of classes and group workshops are available to prisoners, aimed at preparing them for life outside. Many focus on improving self-esteem, controlling drug dependency, and on developing empathy for victims and self-discipline. Inmates without high school diplomas are encouraged to prepare for their General Equivalency Diploma (GED) or for more advanced national educational programs.

THE ROLE OF THE CORRECTIONAL OFFICER

The correctional officer supervises the movement of prisoners to and from work assignments, meals, recreation, and housing units or dormitories. He or she also supervises prisoner work details. It is the duty of the correctional officer to book prisoners upon remand and to operate the security control room. Other duties include assisting with the maintenance of order and discipline, learning and applying techniques of handling unruly and violent prisoners, and using minimum force necessary in resolving situations.

On a daily basis, the correctional officer assists in creating and maintaining an atmosphere conducive to the rehabilitation of a prisoner. The officer is also responsible for conducting routine security checks and inspections, inspecting prisoner quarters, and conducting prisoner counts. He or she is also trained in how to utilize emergency respiratory equipment (gas mask or forced-air respirators) during emergency situations, and will assist in the search for escapees. The officer must react quickly and appropriately to emergencies affecting the safety and security of staff and prisoners.

A correctional officer works two standard shifts. The first is an 84-hour work period consisting of seven 12-hour days followed by seven days off, alternating days and nights. The second type of shift is a 40-hour work period consisting of eight-hour days, five days a week.

All prisons contain a library and computers for inmate use, and all inmates are encouraged to develop vocational skills. The Bureau of Prisons (BOP) offers basic literacy, English as a Second Language (ESL), vocational training, high school equivalency (GED), and university studies. Programs followed for the GED require compulsory attendance for at least 120 days. Sometimes, local state university personnel teach college-level courses. Most prisons have a library system that is part of the state library system, and inmates therefore have access to most of the books that are available in the public libraries. However, in June 1996, the Supreme Court ruled that prisoners' access to law libraries be limited.

A typing room exists in most prisons, where inmates may type letters or write up their journals. Prisoners must use their own typewriter ribbons, purchased in the commissary. Computer or Internet access is rarely permitted in U.S. prisons and is only ever allowed under strict supervision—and then for educational purposes only.

EVENING ROUTINE

During the evening, prisoners are given toilet supplies, soap, and other personal hygiene items needed for the night's use. At 10:00 P.M., another count is performed and records are again compiled at the control center by staff whose job it is to keep up files on the day's activities and statistics. For obvious reasons, every key in the facility must be accounted for, and a complete inventory of handcuffs, tools, and radios is taken. Should even one key be missing, all the locks may be changed.

At 11:00 P.M., patrol officers deliberately set off the detection systems around the perimeter in order to make sure that they are still working. Inmates may play cards or watch TV, but in most prisons, inmates are locked in their cells for the night by 10:00 P.M.

A final count takes place late in the evening, usually at 11:30 P.M., and the lights are turned off for the night. Sometimes, additional counts take place during the night.

DEATH ROW

Although outlawed in many countries around the world, the death penalty for first-degree murder still exists throughout the U.S., and Death Row is a feature of most state and federal prisons, except in Michigan, Rhode Island, and Wisconsin—states that do not have the death penalty. Alaska, Hawaii, Iowa, Maine, Massachusetts, Minnesota, North Dakota, Vermont, West Virginia, and the District of Columbia do not have death-penalty statutes either, and a **moratorium** on executions currently exists in Illinois. Texas is the leader in the use of the death penalty in the U.S.

A typical Death Row cell is 6 feet wide, 9 feet long, and 9.5 feet high.

Death Row inmates are confined to their cells almost continuously, let out for exercise and legal visits only. Many spend their days working on their own cases, as seen here.

CHARACTERISTICS OF THE U.S. PRISON POPULATION

Overwhelmingly, the U.S. prison population is young and male, although women are increasingly being sent to prison. In fact, the population of women inmates has grown faster than that of males. The average age of women in prison is 29, and 58 percent have not finished high school. Almost one out of every three black men between the ages of 20 and 29 is incarcerated, on probation, or on parole. Almost one out of every eight Hispanic men between the ages of 20 and 29 is incarcerated, on probation, or on parole. Black males have a 29 percent chance of serving time in prison at some point in their lives; Hispanic males have a 16 percent chance; white males have a 4 percent chance.

Most inmates have drug and alcohol problems, are illiterate or undereducated, and are unemployed at the time of committing their offenses. Many U.S. inmates have AIDS, hepatitis C, or tuberculosis, usually as a result of drug-addiction habits. Most inmates are from broken families. A large percentage of inmates have parents, siblings, or children who have served time. More than 94 percent of these offenders will eventually be released from prison, but many will re-offend upon their release, usually because of their addiction.

Death Row inmates are awakened at 5:00 A.M. every day for breakfast, and are served meals three times a day. Death Row inmates are confined to their cells constantly, except for exercise and legal visits. The only "contact" visits that Death Row inmates have are with their lawyers, when they sit across a table from each other discussing legal appeals. Most Death Row inmates are not allowed cable television or air conditioning, and generally only two personal phone calls are allowed every day.

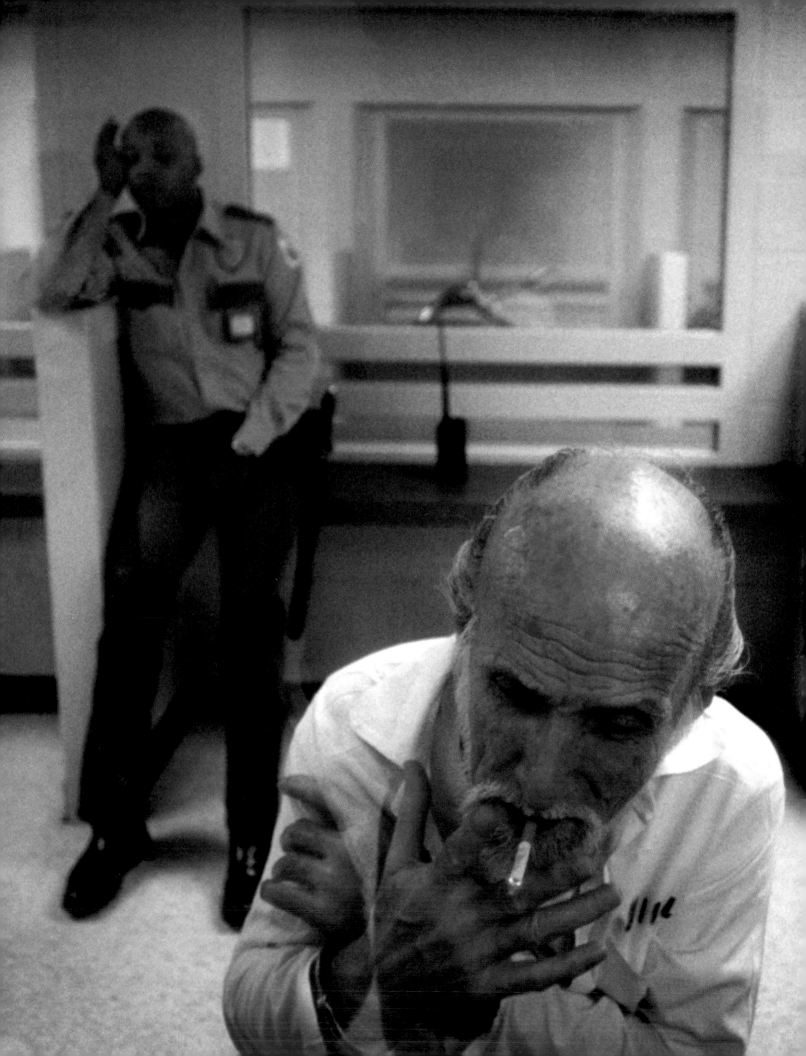

Legal Rights and Visitation

"Tough on crime" policies in the U.S. criminal justice system extend into prison life, and American prisons are extremely intolerant of bad behavior. An internal regime of punishment and reward is practiced in all U.S. prisons and can dramatically increase a prison sentence, although it is unlikely to decrease it by much more than a small margin.

By law, inmates are permitted confidential visits and written and telephone communication with legal counsel. They must be made aware of the existence of appropriate legal documents and information, and are guaranteed reasonable access to them, including within prison libraries. Inmates must be given a reasonable opportunity to seek legal counsel prior to a disciplinary hearing on a serious disciplinary offense, and be provided with information regarding the availability of legal aid services upon request. Should legal aid be unavailable or should the inmate choose not to make use of this service, legal fees must be paid by the inmate, but he or she must have reasonable access to services for photocopying of legal materials.

VISITATION REGULATIONS

Every prison institution has a rigid set of visitation rules. A schedule of regular visitation hours is available to staff, inmates, and visitors, and these are based on each unit's schedule, space, staffing constraints, and other

Left: A long-term Death Row inmate in Arkansas is allowed out of his cell for a cigarette, while a correctional officer stands guard. Death Row inmates are permitted official state or legal visits only and spend much of their time in isolation.

Two maximum-security inmates await visitors at the Oklahoma State Penitentiary. Each visit lasts for up to two hours, but may be terminated at the first sign of inappropriate behavior from either the inmate or visitor.

security or operational-related issues. A visit between an inmate and his or her visitor is generally conducted under staff supervision in an open area, allowing for limited physical contact and movement within the area. Visitors are closely searched for contraband implements; in other words, any item that could be used as an aid to escape or any item that could be used to disguise or alter an inmate's appearance. Cameras, video, audio, or other related equipment are generally not permitted inside the prison.

Some visits are non-contact only, meaning that a prisoner and visitor can meet only through a barrier. This type of visit is generally restricted to any visitor who might attempt to pass drugs to the inmate, and as punishment for bad behavior. Each inmate has a list of approved visitors, consisting of no more than 10 persons and including immediate family members, other relatives, and friends. Prison wardens are responsible for screening and approving visitors and must vigilantly watch for any signs of drug smuggling or suspicious behavior.

Once the new inmate has decided on his or her visitor list, he or she is responsible for sending all potential visitors special application forms, which the designated visitors must complete and return to the prison for validation each time they enter the prison complex. A complete criminal-history background check of the potential visitor is generally fulfilled before any visitor is admitted to the prison. Approved minors, meaning those aged under 10 years, include the inmate's natural, step-, or adopted children, who may visit when accompanied by an approved adult listed on the

At Angola Prison in Louisiana, correctional officers discuss whether or not to remove a Death Row inmate's handcuffs in preparation for a legal visit.

PARENTS IN PRISON

In the U.S., 1.5 million children have a parent in jail or prison; another 3.5 million children have a parent on parole or probation. Over 80 percent of the female prisoners in the United States are mothers, and 70 percent of them are single parents. Two-thirds of incarcerated women in the U.S. have children under the age of 18. Twenty-two percent of all minor children with a parent in prison are under five years old.

inmate's visitation list. Only one inmate may be visited at a time, even though there may be other family members in the same prison facility.

THE DUTY OF THE VISITOR

Visitors are required to register before visiting by completing the daily visitor sign-in sheet at the visitation office. A record is kept of each visitor's complete name and the dates of each visit. An inmate has the right to refuse visitation from anyone, except a Department of Corrections staff member on official business or anyone acting under a court order. An inmate who does refuse visitation with any other persons must complete a visitation waiver for each instance of refusal. Inmates are generally permitted a visit from a maximum of six persons at any one time, regardless of age, during each regular visitation. Often, an infant child may be brought in to visit its mother or father. A privacy screen is made available to let a mother and child share more intimate time together.

Visitation staff may terminate a visit if either the inmate or visitors become aggressive or behave inappropriately, or if they are reasonably suspected of being under the influence of an intoxicant, such as alcohol. Abusive language and any disruptive behavior are not permitted. A brief kiss or an embrace are permitted only at the beginning and end of the visitation period. Visitors are allowed to bring one unopened package of cigarettes in with them, but must only ever use a flame-free electric cigarette lighter. Every visitor is subject to an intensive search, including bags, children's clothing, and baby strollers. Visiting rights for the inmate may be withheld as a form of punishment—for example, for smuggling in items from a visitor or for indecent behavior.

Visitors are usually allowed to visit for up to two hours. Board games, card games, and books are permitted. Prisoners' civil rights have decreased in recent years in many states. By law, prison officials may institute a number of restrictions and punishments, ranging from reduced visiting to bans on television or newspapers.

Work

Work inside prisons for inmates is not compulsory by law. Nevertheless, it is strongly encouraged in American prisons, and forms part of a points system. Because, in general, each day worked reduces a prisoner's sentence by one day, inmates are highly motivated to work. In addition, any prisoners who refuse to work risk certain forms of punishment, such as reduced family visits and limited telephone access.

It is widely believed by state governments as well as the federal government that a regular routine of work for an inmate prevents boredom, provides a productive outlet, and instills a work ethic. Regular work helps prepare the inmate for a useful life outside the prison at the end of his or her sentence and helps to build confidence and self-esteem during the sentence period. For these reasons, American prisons generally insist on prisoner participation in work regimes. Most work that inmates perform takes place within workshops situated within the prison institution, and work is always closely supervised. Only inmates who are nonviolent and who are relatively motivated to work are allowed to work.

Federal Prison Industries (FPI), operating under the trade name Unicor, employs more than 21,000 federal inmates. Approximately 60 percent of its contracts are with the Pentagon, and products such as uniforms, filing cabinets, electronic equipment, and military helmets are sold to the Pentagon and to other federal agencies.

In some states, including California, inmates are surveyed for a wide range of work skills before they are placed in prison. In other words, an

Left: At a "boot camp" in Illinois, inmates carry logs around the compound as part of an exercise in motivational training. Such a task is typical of the boot camp's emphasis on challenging activities that require physical and mental discipline.

effort is made to match skilled inmates to prisons where their skills will be valued. At the same time, inmates with lower-grade skills are encouraged to upgrade their skills and to learn new trades.

Examples of different kinds of prison industry include making clothing, working in the prison laundry, making furniture for the prison and its offices, assembling electronic parts for appliances, and manufacturing a range of products, from shoes and detergents, to stationery products. A major occupation in many prisons is stamping license plates for use within the state in which the prison is located. In women's prisons, the type of work differs, tending to be geared more towards work in textiles, laundry, telemarketing, record keeping, and data entry.

Inmates at Auburn Correctional Facility in New York manufacture state license plates. Prisons provide employment to foster cooperation and teamwork.

A chain gang in Alabama prepares to cut overgrown grass along Interstate 65. Chain gangs working outdoors have been a common sight in Alabama since they were reintroduced in the mid-1990s. Several other U.S. states have also adopted this form of enforced labor.

WORKING OUTSIDE OF PRISON WALLS

Minimum-security prisoners are sometimes taken out of the prison to work at the plants of such companies as Honda, Konica, Microsoft, and Toys R Us. Occasionally, prison labor is used during industrial strikes in an area. In California and Oregon, prison-made clothing competes successfully with producers in both Latin America and Asia, and also enjoys an export market. In Texas, Wackenhut, the private prison-based company has even won high-tech industry contracts from metropolitan areas and uses inmate labor to produce electrical parts.

Work in rural prisons sometimes extends to the operation of farms, dairies, slaughterhouses, and meat-packing plants. Vegetables and fruit are

Inmates break concrete blocks that will then be used to prevent land erosion on a lakeshore. Inmates carry out many useful outdoor maintenance jobs throughout the U.S. They also often provide valuable additional labor during natural disasters, such as forest fires or floods.

sold wholesale to local restaurants or to state agencies. Teams of prison inmates can easily be assembled at short notice for seasonal and short-demand work, such as picking fruit, so a prison will often volunteer field crews to assist in local harvests. In northeastern states and in cities that suffer winter blizzards, prison **chain gangs** are sometimes used to shovel snow from the roads and to clear public pathways. For example, the city of Buffalo in New York is blizzard-prone and regularly takes advantage of this form of readily available manpower.

In some southwestern states, inmates work as part of the state's fire control and forest conservation teams, using field camps as their work base. In California, for example, there are 33 male conservation camps and 3 female conservation camps, all specifically designed to provide additional wildland firefighting crews. Most prisoners value the chance to take part in this kind of work, despite the dangers entailed. Field camps of this kind are lower security and allow inmates to play a useful role in the community.

THE CHAIN GANG AND PRISONER'S RIGHTS

Chain gangs were introduced after the Civil War, when slavery had become illegal, as a form of slave labor, but were outlawed in the U.S. during the 1950s. Alabama was the first state to reintroduce the chain gang in 1995.

Today, Alabama is the state that most regularly uses the controversial chain gang method of prison labor, reintroduced to the United States in the mid-1990s. As part of a chain gang, inmates are shackled together in leg irons and chains to perform tasks of physical labor. Only nonviolent inmates are allowed to work as part of a chain gang, and work periods do not usually last longer than 30 days.

Prisoners are not allowed to form unions or to negotiate increased wages. They do not have the right to strike or to call meetings. Occasionally, an inmate may file a lawsuit if he or she has a serious complaint about work. Prisoners are paid the going wage for jobs that they do. This usually translates to the minimum wage, and the state is generally entitled to

TYPES OF PRISON WORK

The work available in prison comes in a variety of forms. Prisoners can find employment performing such duties as:

- **Construction of new facilities**
- **Agricultural work, such as growing vegetables or vegetable food-processing**
- **Meat cutting**
- **Cleaning up blizzard or hurricane damage**
- **Metal-shop work**
- **Repairing and making office furniture**
- **Making clothing**
- **Stamping license plates**
- **Microcomputer systems technology work**
- **Optics**
- **Telemarketing and data entry**
- **Maintenance work around the prison**

withhold about 80 percent of the earnings in order to fund telephone expenses and other added benefits within the prison system. Most prisoners earn little more than $10.00 a day. However, work is valuable to all inmates because it helps to reduce their overall prison sentence.

Prison labor does, however, entail the risk of inmate escape. In fact, this is how prisoners most commonly manage to escape. Sometimes, even seemingly motivated, hard-working, and willing inmates entrusted to responsible posts will deceive prison staff, feigning cooperation and motivation in order to plot their escape. For this reason, all work in prison must be carefully supervised, and any potential for abuse within the prison work system must be closely monitored.

Women in a chain gang in Arizona burying the dead at a local cemetery. Once seen as inhumane, chain gangs have made a comeback and enable inmates to work outdoors without any risk of escape or threat of harm to the general public.

Violence and Gang Warfare

The consequences of bad behavior within prisons are serious. Drug dealing, taking part in a fight, or making a violent threat against a prison official may add years to an inmate's sentence.

Prison culture has its own rules, customs, and language. Prisoners may clash for political, **ethnic**, or simply personal reasons. By law, corrections officers are duty-bound to protect inmates from each other, and struggle to prevent abuse. However, prison populations are notoriously devious and unpredictable. The potential for violence is never far away in prison, and much abuse between prisoners goes undetected.

The role of ethnicity is important in prison management. Ethnic- or gang-based hatred can run deep. Corrections officers try to keep known enemies away from each other, particularly in the recreation yard or workshop, but they may not always be aware of less-obvious **vendettas** or that an inmate may be in serious danger.

If a prisoner feels vulnerable, he or she may ask to be placed in protective custody. In such cases, the inmate is usually moved to a segregated housing and work area while the cause for his or her concern is investigated. An inmate in such a situation is expected to identify his or her enemy and to provide all relevant information that may be used against the perpetrator in

Left: As part of an anti-gang initiative, a former gang member has one of his gang tattoos burned off in a minor medical procedure. Prison gangs cause violence and operate drug- and weapon-dealing rings, and intergang warfare can trigger wholesale prison riots. Gang membership is strongly discouraged by the prison authorities.

a disciplinary situation. Clearly, all cases must be thoroughly investigated and supported by means of reliable evidence, because the risk of framing someone or **slander** is high.

Special protective housing units are maintained in most state and federal prisons for inmates who cannot be accommodated in the prison system for reasons of security. However, special protective housing units are generally used as a last resort. This means that the inmate who is being victimized

A Californian gang member demonstrates the secret signal used by his gang. His gang "boss" is currently on Death Row facing execution for murder.

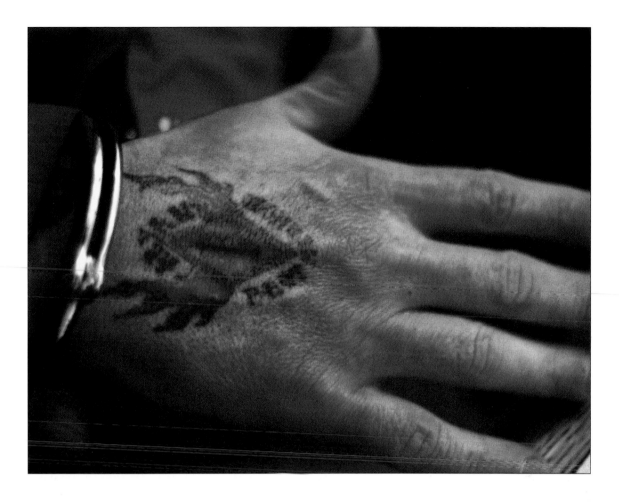

A Death Row inmate in Delaware shows off his Ayran Brotherhood tattoo. His left hand is tattooed with a neo-Nazi swastika. Originating in the 1960s, Ayran Brotherhood is one of the biggest prison gangs in the country and preaches white supremacy.

will be subjected to repeated violence or threats before corrections officers finally take preventive action and place him or her in the special protective housing unit. The most common solution to any threatening situation is to move a prisoner to another institution altogether.

PRISON GANGS

There are two different types of gangs that may operate within prisons: street gangs that enter the prison from the outside world, and prison gangs established for mutual protection and to control various things within the system. Common prison gangs in the U.S. today include Aryan

The recreation area at Huntsville Prison, Texas. Recreation periods are a time of high security risk, and correctional officers are always on the lookout for suspicious activities and any signs of either drug or weapon smuggling or dealing.

Brotherhood, the Black Guerrilla Family, Neta, Neustra Familia, the Mexican Mafia (EME), and the Texas Syndicate.

Aryan Brotherhood (AB) originated in 1967 in the San Quentin State Prison, California Department of Corrections. AB is a white supremacist, neo-Nazi gang. Its symbols are the shamrock, swastikas, double lighting bolts, and the numbers "666." AB is affiliated with the Mexican Mafia (EME) and therefore opposes the EME's long-time enemy, the La Nuestra Familia (NF). The Aryan Brotherhood fosters racial hatred, and its enemies include the Black Guerrilla Family (BGF), the Crips, and the Bloods.

The Black Guerrilla Family was founded in 1966 at San Quentin State Prison, California, by a former Black Panther member named George L. Jackson. It is a Marxist/Maoist/Leninist revolutionary organization that is extremely antigovernment. Among its symbols are depictions of crossed sabers and shotgun, and a black dragon overtaking a prison or prison tower. Enemies include Aryan Brotherhood, Texas Syndicate, Aryan Brotherhood of Texas, and Mexican Mafia. It is allied with La Nuestra Familia and is supported by many black street gangs.

The Neta was established in 1970 in Rio Pedras Prison, Puerto Rico, and it also has strong ties to street gangs. Its members are strongly patriotic and are associated with a revolutionary Puerto Rican group called Los Macheteros. Neta colors are red, white, and blue, and members usually display the Puerto Rican flag. Enemy gangs include the Latin Kings and Los Solidos.

La Nuestra Familia (NF) originated in Soledad Prison in California in the mid-1960s and was originally formed to protect rural Hispanics from the urban Mexican Mafia (EME). Symbols include identifying red rags, large black tattoos, and a sombrero with a dagger. The Mexican Mafia is their chief rival, but Aryan Brotherhood is another major rival.

Mexican Mafia was formed in the late '50s from an urban Los Angeles street gang and is an ethnic solidarity gang. Its symbols are the initials "EME," the Mexican flag, a single handprint, usually black in color—the

EME symbol of eternal war—and the initials "MM" or "M." Its main enemy is La Nuestra Familia. Because members in both these gangs have vowed to kill each other on sight, the federal Bureau of Prisons has adopted a policy of absolute separation of confirmed members.

The Texas Syndicate originated in Folsom Prison, in California, in the early '70s. People must usually be a Texas native to be a member, but the TS does also accept members from Latin American countries, such as Colombia, Cuba, and Mexico. Symbols include tattoos with a "TS" in the design, and its enemies are Aryan Brotherhood, La Nuestra Familia, and Mexican Mafia.

In addition to these major prison gangs are numerous other prison networks of urban gangs from the streets of New York City, Chicago, and Los Angeles.

GANG ASSOCIATIONS AND ACTIVITIES

Most gang activity centers on drug trafficking, **extortion**, pressure rackets, and internal discipline. Known gang members are usually housed in "super-maximum" prisons, and during admission, corrections officers try hard to determine whether or not an inmate is a gang member. They will look for tattoos, written material, photos, and any signs of association with known gang members. Any determined gang association carries serious consequences for the inmate's sentencing and treatment within prison because prison gang members are thought to join gangs for life.

An inmate who is identified as a gang member must undergo a debriefing process in which he or she is ordered to provide specific information on gang activities (including names of other gang members) and pass a polygraph. Debriefing can take a long period of time and may involve numerous interrogations over a protracted period of time until prison officials have extracted the necessary information. An inmate who is falsely identified as a gang member will quickly reveal him- or herself in the debriefing process as being ignorant of gang codes and so on.

VIOLENCE IN PRISON

Violence is a major problem in prisons, and nearly two percent of prison inmates are held in protective custody nationally. In spite of these measures, prisoner violence and gang-related incidents result in a number of deaths in prisons every year. In 1998, for example, 79 inmates were killed nationally in the U.S. and many thousands more were injured severely enough to require medical attention.

Prison riots usually take place in protest against inmate conditions and when relations between correctional officers and inmates have broken down. The first prison riot in the U.S. was in 1774 at Newgate Prison in Connecticut. More recent riots include incidents at Attica (New York) in 1971, Santa Fe (New Mexico) in 1980, Atlanta (Georgia) and Oakdale, Los Angeles (California) in 1989, and Lucasville (Ohio) in 1993.

Getting Out

An inmate's earliest possible release date (EPRD) is computed by a formula that takes into account the number of days served, the time left under the sentence, and the amount of credit in the behavior points system that has been earned or lost for good or bad behavior. Inmates are informed of their EPRD by way of periodic status sheets.

COMPASSIONATE RELEASE AND PAROLE

Sometimes, if an inmate becomes ill—for example, with AIDS—the possibility of death before the end of the sentence becomes a reason to apply for compassionate release. Ultimately, the power to award a compassionate release rests with the state or federal Department of Corrections. Several factors are considered, including: the inmate is terminally ill with a life expectancy of six months or less; the term was for a violent or sexual offense; and there are family and community resources that can care for an individual. Sometimes, it is difficult to judge the life expectancy of a seriously ill inmate, and the risk of misdiagnosis is therefore high. For the authorities, the worst-case scenario is clearly that an inmate released on compassionate release will go on to commit another crime while on compassionate-release probation.

Most inmates in U.S. prisons are incarcerated for drug-related offenses and will eventually be released on parole. In the state of California, parole is mandatory and always follows a term of imprisonment. Once an inmate is due for parole, he or she is given an official notice and informed of the conditions of parole so that he or she can sign for release. Inmates who do not sign risk having

Left: Released after 14 years of incarceration, a former inmate celebrates his newfound freedom and embraces his private investigator and attorney.

extra years added to their sentence. However undesirable the conditions of parole may seem, inmates are usually advised by their attorney or public defender to agree to the conditions without objection, or risk facing the revocation of their parole, or, worse still, a renewed sentence.

Conditions of parole are designed to anticipate and limit the possibility of further crimes. If, for example, the inmate has shown signs of mental instability, one of the conditions of parole may be that he or she receive psychiatric treatment upon release, including psychotropic medication. Parole conditions may also specify limits on certain jobs or occupations or from associating with certain people. For example, anyone convicted for any kind of child molestation offense would be told not to pursue any kind of job working with or near children. Gang members may be instructed in their parole conditions to avoid contact with former gang associates. Most commonly, parole often requires narcotics testing or participation in drug-rehabilitation group programs.

PAROLE REVOCATION

Any inmate who breaks the rules of his or her parole in the first year may have his or her parole revoked. In other words, if he or she breaks the conditions of his or her parole, he or she will have to go to a special hearing and may be returned to prison for specific periods of time.

Breaking parole is relatively commonplace for those who have committed drug offenses, because chemical addiction can make it difficult for someone out on parole to avoid re-offending. Such a person may have his or her parole revoked at any time for psychiatric treatment.

In this case, the person on parole need not have actively committed any misconduct. Rather, he or she is considered to suffer from a mental disorder that makes him or her a potential danger, either to others or to him- or herself. If no treatment within the community is available or is deemed appropriate, the person on parole may be sent to a psychiatric prison in order to receive treatment.

The celebrity baseball player Darryl Strawberry, incarcerated for drug-related offenses, apologizes to court for his parole violations. Parole conditions must be observed, and participation in drug rehabilitation programs is usually mandatory.

LIFE PRISONERS

Inmates serving life sentences have little or no hope of being released on parole. In the rare instance that a convincing case for parole is made, the state governor retains the right to reject parole. It has to be said that, in most cases, a combination of politics and public disapproval makes it impossible for life prisoners, even those who have undergone massive personal change, to be released on parole. These prisoners must therefore come to terms with the fact that they will grow old and eventually die behind bars.

A young inmate discusses his parole plans with a counselor. Understanding and observing parole conditions maximizes an offender's chances of avoiding a further prison sentence. Many young offenders need constant guidance from the authorities and parole officers to avoid re-offending.

Released! Former Death Row inmate Roberto Miranda carries his belongings after he was released from the Clark County Detention Center, Texas, in 1996. Earlier, a judge had dismissed capital murder charges against him based on new evidence.

RELEASE

Unfortunately, transition from prison to the outside world is a largely neglected area. Inmates are often released on parole without a home to go to and with a diminished network of support in the outside world. Marriages may have broken down, caring parents and grandparents may have died, and whole communities may have changed beyond recognition. The recently released inmate generally finds him- or herself facing anxiety and isolation in the outside world, and will experience a lasting social stigma. Although halfway houses or homeless shelters exist, they are often hotbeds of crime. Most ex-prisoners find it extremely difficult to find work because a prison record is almost guaranteed to put off any prospective employer. Few programs exist to help ex-prisoners find jobs after prison. Gang members are often quickly drawn back into their old community and its vices. Old **enmities** may be settled by violent or vengeful means.

Active prison ministries struggle hard to provide support at the release stage. Some of the most effective ministries are those that help ex-offenders find work within the community. Such communities are, however, rare, and many ex-offenders will either become homeless or will, despite the hardship and deprivation suffered during their prison sentence, return to an active life of crime, lacking any other employment opportunity.

Prisoners can be released for a number of reasons, including parole. Parole is always awarded with fixed conditions: the prisoner has to behave well and not break the law after his or her release.

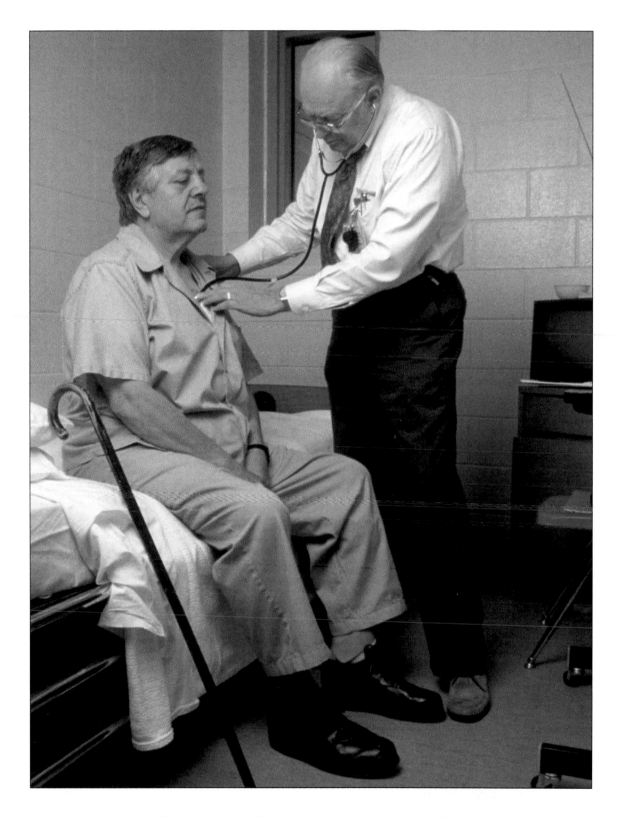

An inmate in poor health receives a medical examination from a prison doctor. By the time he is released, he will probably be too infirm to work. Unfortunately, many who leave prison in advanced years face loneliness and poverty beyond the prison walls.

GLOSSARY

Chain gang: a group of convicts chained together used to perform physical labor

Commissary: a store for equipment and provisions

Conspiracy: planning with other people to commit an unlawful act (often for political motives)

Enmity: mutual hatred

Epidemic: excessively prevalent

Ethnic: having specific cultural traditions

Extortion: the act of obtaining money from a person by force, intimidation, or undue or illegal power

Felony: a crime considered serious enough that it must be punished by imprisonment

Gothic: an architectural style reflecting the influence of the medieval Gothic, a style of building dating from 12th-century Europe

Incarcerate: to imprison

Inventory: a detailed list

Misdemeanor: a crime that need not be punished by imprisonment, or that merits a short sentence only

Money laundering: to transfer illegally obtained money through an outside party to conceal the true source

Moratorium: a suspension of activity set by an authority

Parole: when an inmate is conditionally released before his or her sentence is served, on strict condition that he or she report regularly to a parole officer

Penitentiary: a state or federal prison in the U.S.

Probation: the action of suspending the sentence of a convicted offender and giving the offender freedom for good behavior under the supervision of a probation officer

Racketeering: to conduct a fraudulent scheme or business activity

Recession: a period of reduced economic activity

Regimen: a systematic plan designed to bring benefits as it is carried out

Slander: a false and defamatory oral statement about a person

Tiered: having several layers

Vendetta: an often prolonged series of retaliatory, vengeful, or hostile acts or exchange of such acts

CHRONOLOGY

1830s: Most U.S. states begin to build their first prisons.

1851: California establishes a state prison system in response to increased criminal activity during the Gold Rush.

1891: The Three Prisons Act establishes the federal prison system and builds its first three prisons at Leavenworth, Kansas; Atlanta, Georgia; and on McNeil Island in Washington State.

1930s: Prison labor used in war effort; Federal Prison Industries is established to provide training and paid work to inmates.

1946: Alcatraz Prison "Blast Out" leaves two officers and three inmates dead.

1950s: The chain gang is abolished in every state.

1965: The Prisoner Rehabilitation Act makes halfway houses and work/study release available by law to U.S. prisoners for the first time.

1970: Arkansas prison system is ruled unconstitutional.

1971: Attica Prison Riot, New York State; 50 people were taken as hostages, 10 of whom died, including six correctional officers; 32 inmates also died.

1972: Nixon declares a "War on Drugs."

1984: President Ronald Reagan revives the "War on Drugs" with the "Zero Tolerance" and "Just Say No!" campaigns.

1987: Severe Atlanta federal prison riots.

1989: The federal prison population reaches 53,000.

1995: One hundred fifty new prisons are built in the United States, and 171 existing prisons are expanded.

1995: Alabama's governor Fob James reinstates the chain gang system.

1996: September 27, riot at New Folsom leaves one prisoner dead and 13 injured after fighting between Latino and African-American prisoners; April, President Clinton signs The Prison Litigation Reform Act (PLRA) into law; the PLRA is designed to limit prisoners' access to federal courts due to allegedly frivolous lawsuits.

1997: The federal prison population reaches 100,000.

2000: The total U.S. prison population reaches 2,000,000 inmates.

2001: June 11, Oklahoma City bomber Timothy McVeigh was put to death by lethal injection, the first federal prisoner to be executed in 38 years.

FURTHER INFORMATION

Useful Web Sites

Bureau of Prisons home page: www.bop.gov/

Bureau of Justice Department Statistics, Prison Statistics:
www.ojp.usdoj.gov/bjs/prisons.htm

The National Institute of Corrections:
www.nicic.org/about/divisions/prisons.htm

Prison Legal News: www.prisonlegalnews.org/

Correctional News: www.correctionalnews.com/

The Corrections Connections Network: www.corrections.com/

Human Rights Watch Prison Group: www.hrw.org/prisons/

The Other Side of the Wall: www.prisonwall.org/

The International Center for Prison Studies:
www.kcl.ac.uk/depsta/rel/icps/home.html

Further Reading

Abbott, Jack Henry. *In the Belly of the Beast: Letters from Prison*. New York: Vintage Books, 1991.

Bergner, Daniel. *God of the Rodeo: The Quest for Redemption in Louisiana's Angola Prison*. New York: Ballantine Books, 1999.

Champion, Dean J. *Corrections in the United States: A Contemporary Perspective*. Upper Saddle River, NJ: Prentice Hall, 2001.

Chevigny, Bell Gale, American Center of P.E.N., and Helen Prejean. *Doing Time: 25 Years of Prison Writing—A PEN American Center Prize Anthology*. New York: Dist. by Time Warner Trade Pub., 1999.

Evans, Jeff (Editor); Jimmy Santiago Baca (foreword); and Craig W. Haney, (afterword). *Undoing Time: American Prisoners in Their Own Words*. Boston: Northeastern University Press, 2000.

Girshick, Lori B. *No Safe Haven: Stories of Women in Prison.* Boston: Northeastern University Press, 2000.

Hogshire, Jim. *You Are Going To Prison.* Port Townsend, Washington: Breakout Productions, 1999.

Wicker, Tom and Bruce H. Franklin (editor). *Prison Writing: In 20th-Century America.* New York: Penguin USA, 1998.

Wideman, John Edgar. *Brothers and Keepers.* New York: Vintage Books, 1995.

Williams, "Tookie" and Barbara Cottman Becnel. *Life In Prison.* New York: Morrow Junior Books, 1998.

Wynn, Jennifer. *Inside Rikers: Stories from the World's Largest Penal Colony.* New York: St. Martin's Press, 2001.

About the Author

Joanna Rabiger was born in London, England, and was educated at Cambridge University and Columbia College, Chicago. She has worked for the London-based publishers Cassell and The Womens' Press, and in the editorial division of the trade books department at Oxford University Press. In 1999, she moved to the U.S. to train as a film editor at Columbia College, Chicago, concentrating on documentary work. She now works as a freelance writer and documentary film editor in Austin, Texas. While a film student in Chicago, Joanna also worked as a researcher for the Emmy award-winning documentary production company Nomadic Pictures. For Nomadic she contributed developmental production work on a TV series on women public defenders and the U.S. criminal justice system, and researched the role of prison ministries and support systems for recently released prisoners, covering such topics as race, incarcerated parents and their children, drug rehabilitation, halfway houses, employment issues, and re-offending.

INDEX